Inspiring Stories for Brilliant Boys

Mr & Mrs Wolf

Note: This book was previously released under the title *Leo Teo Tales*. It features a brand-new story and has undergone revisions based on feedback from readers, ensuring an enhanced and improved experience.

Table of Contents

Introduction

Hello, amazing reader, thank you for selecting our book to read. We believe that every child holds the potential to be the hero of their own story, and our book is dedicated to nurturing the self-belief essential for that journey. Drawing inspiration from real-life kids, our characters and their relationships are authentic and relatable, capturing moments of joy, sadness, and everything in between. These tales go beyond mere entertainment; they are designed to inspire and motivate, encouraging young readers to cultivate traits such as empathy, bravery, and resilience as they navigate their own adventures.

We aim to provide young minds with blueprints for facing their own challenges by presenting stories where characters triumph over conflicts. Through these pages, we hope to evoke a range of emotions—from courage and determination to empathy and gratitude. Our ultimate goal is to leave a lasting impact, empowering every young reader to be brave, thoughtful, and resilient. Dive into these heartwarming tales and allow them to inspire the hero within.

Happy reading!

The Best Christmas Ever

Oliver was only six, but he could play the piano like someone twice his age. Whenever he played, the kids in the neighborhood gathered around to watch. Even the adults couldn't help but smile and nod along. His parents were so proud of him that one day his dad surprised him with a beautiful, big piano that now sat in their basement.

The piano became Oliver's treasure. Every day after school, he'd run straight to it and play until dinner, his little sister Melody, who was only two, sometimes watching him with curious eyes. She didn't understand the music, but she loved sitting beside him and tapping the keys with her tiny fingers.

One evening, while showing off a new tune, Oliver got an idea. What if I taught Melody how to play? It would be a Christmas surprise for everyone if she could play "Jingle Bells." The thought filled him with excitement.

"When you play the 'Jingle Bells' tune, everyone will be amazed!" Oliver whispered to her with a grin.

"Jin-go Bells!" Melody repeated, her chubby face lighting up.

"But shhh, it has to be a secret," he added, holding a finger to his lips.

Oliver decided to teach Melody at night, when their parents went for their evening walk. The next night, as soon as he heard the front door close, he snuck into Melody's room and gently lifted her out of bed.

"Come on, Melo! It's piano time," he whispered.

They tiptoed to the basement, and Oliver sat her on the piano bench beside him. Melody squealed with excitement and immediately slapped her hands down on the keys, creating a loud, jumbled noise.

"That's a bad song, Melo!" he chuckled, covering his ears.

He placed her fingers on one key. "Watch me. You have to press one key at a time, like this." He played the first note of "Jingle Bells," and it sounded soft and lovely. But as soon as he lifted her hand, she went right back to smacking her little fists on every key.

"Come on, Melo," he groaned. "Christmas is only a week away. You have to focus!"

Just then, a thought struck him. Did I leave the garage door open? Worried, he darted upstairs to check. Halfway up the steps, he heard Melody banging on the keys again, loud enough to make the walls vibrate.

"Oh no," he muttered, realizing the noise would echo throughout the neighborhood. He turned to rush back down but stopped when he saw the porch light flick on at Mrs. Clinton's house. Mrs. Clinton was known for her strictness and quick temper. All the kids knew to avoid making noise around her.

"Oh no," Oliver whispered to himself, watching as Mrs. Clinton stepped outside, her face already crinkled with annoyance. Oliver grabbed Melody by the hand and hurried her upstairs

Within moments, there was a loud, steady knock at their door. "Mr. Peters! Open the door!" Mrs. Clinton shouted.

By then, Oliver's parents had just returned from their walk. Oliver, trying to act casual, opened the door, attempting to block Melody from view.

"Mrs. Clinton," he said with a sheepish grin.

Mrs. Clinton looked over Oliver's head and glared. "The noise! I was in the middle of my yoga session when the racket started. I nearly fell out of a tree pose!"

Oliver's dad stepped in. "Oh, Mrs. Clinton, we're so sorry! It must've been, uh...TV noises?" He glanced down at Oliver for backup.

"Yes! I was watching TV," Oliver said quickly, his eyes darting back to Melody, who had wandered over with a cookie she'd swiped from the kitchen.

"Oliver, no more late-night TV and snacks," his mom scolded. "And off to bed, both of you."

Mrs. Clinton huffed, her arms folded. "TV noises... Well, it better not happen again. Goodnight." She spun on her heel and headed back to her house.

As Oliver and Melody returned to their rooms, he realized that teaching her without getting caught would be harder than he thought. But he wasn't giving up.

The next day, while playing with Melody, Oliver noticed her love for candies, especially the tangy ones. That's it! he thought, hatching a new plan. He placed a candy on each key he wanted her to press, starting with the "Jingle Bells" tune.

Each time she picked up a candy, she pressed a note. And before long, Melody was unknowingly playing the right notes. For the next few days, Oliver repeated this trick, sneaking Melody down to the basement every night after their parents left. Slowly but surely, Melody got the hang of it, sometimes even pressing the keys without a candy reward.

A night before Christmas, Oliver and Melody snuck down for one final practice. "Okay, Melo, let's play it one more time," he said, pulling out a bag of candies. But before he could set them up, Melody placed her fingers on the keys and began pressing the right notes, one by one, without his help.

Oliver's eyes widened. "You're doing it!" he shouted, jumping up in excitement and accidentally spilling candies everywhere. "Oops," he chuckled, bending down to pick them up.

One candy rolled across the floor into the laundry room. Determined to retrieve every candy, Oliver followed it inside. As he picked up the candy, the door suddenly shut behind him, locking him inside the dark room.

"Oh no, it's locked!" he exclaimed, tugging at the doorknob. "Melody! Can you hear me?"

Outside the door, Melody heard his muffled voice. "Oli?" she whimpered, her lower lip trembling.

"It's okay, Melo. I'll be out soon. Just stay close!" he called out, trying to sound calm.

Suddenly, he heard a loud crash. Melody, trying to reach the candies on a high shelf, had knocked over a flowerpot. His heart raced, knowing there were sharp pieces of glass on the floor.

"Melo, don't move!" he called, panic creeping into his voice. He needed a way to get her away from the glass.

"Okay, Melo, I need you to play the 'bad song' on the piano," he called out. "Remember? Make it super loud, and I'll give you more candies!"

Though puzzled, Melody toddled over to the piano and banged her little fists down, creating the loud, chaotic sound that Mrs. Clinton hated.

Hearing the racket, Mrs. Clinton peered out of her window, her face wrinkling with disapproval. What are they up to now? she thought as she marched over to their house.

Finding the door unlocked, Mrs. Clinton entered and followed the noise to the basement, where she found Melody at the piano. Her stern gaze softened slightly when she saw the little girl surrounded by candy and glass.

"Melody?" Mrs. Clinton called out, surprised. Then she heard a faint voice from behind the laundry room door. "Mrs. Clinton! I'm stuck!"

With a sigh, she opened the door, and Oliver stumbled out, wide-eyed and relieved. Without a second thought, he hugged both Melody and expressed his gratitude to Mrs Clinton. "Thank you, Mrs. Clinton! You saved us!"

Their parents arrived just in time to witness the scene, listening as Mrs. Clinton lectured them gently. "These kids are God's gifts, you know," she said firmly. "They need watching over, especially when they're up to mischief!"

Once she'd left, Oliver's parents turned to him, eyebrows raised. "Anything you'd like to tell us?" his dad asked.

Realizing his plan was out, Oliver sheepishly explained everything. "I just… I just wanted to teach Melody a Christmas song."

His parents were quiet for a moment, and Oliver's heart sank. But then his mom hugged him. "We're proud of you, Ollie. This might be a bit sneaky, but you put your heart into it."

The next day on Christmas eve , friends and neighbors gathered at their home for Christmas. With everyone watching, Melody sat at the piano, and with Oliver's encouragement, began to play "Jingle Bells." Each note was soft but clear, filling the room with the familiar, joyful tune.

As she finished, the guests erupted into applause, and Oliver's parents pulled him into a tight hug. Oliver beamed, feeling prouder than ever, knowing they had just shared the best Christmas memory they could have hoped for.

What a nice story! Even Mrs. Clinton had a heartwarming moment.

I know, right? Bet even she didn't see that coming!

Speaking of surprises... what do you think Mrs. Clinton's favorite holiday movie is?

I dunno... The Grinch?

Nah, Home Alone. Because it's nice and quiet!

14

In a neighborhood where every day was an adventure waiting to happen, Andy and Ruth were inseparable companions. Their shared love for outdoor sports like basketball, baseball, and soccer forged a bond as strong as steel. But above all, it was skateboarding that truly ignited their passion. They glided through the streets with unmatched finesse, earning the admiration of their peers.

When news of an upcoming interschool competition reached their ears, excitement mingled with uncertainty in their hearts. Amidst the myriad of sports on offer — team classics like American football or soccer, or the finesse of individual games like badminton or table tennis — they found themselves at a crossroads.

It was Ruth, with her boundless creativity and thirst for adventure, who proposed a daring idea. "Why don't we try something completely new?" she suggested, her eyes alight with anticipation. "Let's choose a sport we've never attempted before. It'll be a chance for us to showcase not just our athleticism but our intelligence too."

Andy's gaze lit up with excitement at the prospect. "That sounds like a challenge worth taking on," he grinned. "Count me in!"

And so, with a shared sense of determination, they settled on roller skating — a sport as unfamiliar as it was thrilling. With trepidation and excitement coursing through their veins, they strapped on their newly bought skates and ventured onto the smooth expanse of the practice ground, where their other classmates had been practicing for years.

Their initial attempts were met with a series of tumbles and wobbles as they struggled to get up on their feet without falling. Seeing them struggle, Tad, one of their classmates, taunted, "Look at Andy and Ruth! They're like newborn foals trying to stand!" Ruth's confidence instantly faltered.

But Andy, undeterred by the jeers, flashed Ruth a reassuring smile. "Don't let them get to you," he urged, his voice brimming with determination. "We'll get better with practice, I promise."

In an attempt to lighten the mood, Andy tried to get up on his feet by jumping on, but his attempt ended in a spectacular fall, with his legs splitting apart. The laughter swelled, and Tad and his friends started gliding around Andy and Ruth, causing doubt to creep into Ruth's mind. "Maybe we should rethink our choice of sport," she suggested tentatively, her enthusiasm dampened by the mockery.

But Andy remained resolute, his eyes gleaming with determination. "No way," he declared firmly. "We're not just doing this to win. We're doing it because we enjoy it. Remember?"

As their practice session came to an end, Ruth, with a heavy heart, started to leave. Andy asked, "Let's do one more session tomorrow morning. What do you say?"

Ruth sighed and replied, "I'm not coming tomorrow. I'm gonna play volleyball, I guess."

Andy inquired, "But why, Ruth?" Ruth chose to stay silent, leaving Andy to grapple with his own doubts.

Now Andy trudged home; the weight of his bruised knees matched the heaviness in his heart. Each step felt like a burden, a reminder of his disappointment. He slumped his shoulders, the vibrant energy he usually carried replaced by a somber demeanor. His usually upbeat strides were now replaced by a slow, defeated shuffle.

At home, his mother noticed his downcast expression and the way he gingerly touched his bruised knees. "How was your day, Andy?" she asked gently, sensing his despondency.

With a heavy sigh, Andy recounted the events of the day, from the mockery of his classmates to the doubts that had crept into his mind. "I don't think I'll ever get the hang of roller skating," he lamented, his voice tinged with frustration.

His mother listened attentively, her heart aching for her son's disappointment. But instead of dwelling on his failures, she offered words of comfort and wisdom. "Andy, falling over and over again while trying is okay," she said softly, her voice filled with warmth and encouragement. "But falling and never getting up is not okay. You're resilient, and I know you can overcome this challenge. Keep trying your best, and remember to have fun along the way."

With renewed determination, Andy faced the new day with a newfound sense of purpose. The sunrise painted the sky with hues of pink and gold, signaling a fresh start. Inspired by his mother's words, he approached his practice session with renewed vigor. With each attempt, he fell less frequently, his confidence growing with each successful glide.

Andy felt stronger and more determined about roller skating with each passing day, although he still couldn't avoid falling with a split-leg maneuver now and then. Tad and his friends continued to mock him, skating effortlessly around him. In practice matches, Andy often finished last, and the even bigger problem was that he completed his last lap much after everyone else had finished.

Yet, with each passing day, Andy got faster and faster. Even though his iconic fall would derail him, he kept pushing forward.

As the day of the competition arrived, Andy found himself amidst a throng of eager participants. Spotting Ruth excelling in the volleyball competition, he offered her a supportive nod, silently wishing her luck.

Approaching Andy, Ruth sought reassurance about his preparation. With a confident smile, Andy affirmed his readiness, his eyes alight with determination. "I've got this," he assured her, his voice steady and resolute.

Ruth's brow furrowed in confusion as Andy admitted, "I don't mind falling anymore." Her puzzlement lingered, overshadowed by the imminent start of the competition.

As the roller-skating competition commenced, Andy took his place among the other contestants, including Tad, his heart pounding with excitement and nerves. With a determined expression, he pushed off from the starting line, his skates gliding smoothly over the surface of the track. As the race progressed, Andy found himself in a favorable position, steadily maintaining his place near the front of the pack.

However, as the finish line drew nearer, Andy's lead was suddenly threatened by two formidable opponents, one of them being Tad. Their determined expressions mirrored his own. With each passing moment, they gained ground, their skates slicing through the air with effortless speed.

In a daring move, Andy intentionally wobbled and fell, executing his signature split-leg maneuver with precision. The unexpected tactic caught his opponents off guard, allowing him to regain his momentum and surge ahead. With a burst of speed, he crossed the finish line, victorious in his unorthodox approach.

The applause of the crowd washed over him like a wave; their cheers were a symphony of celebration. Even Ruth, who had once doubted his abilities, looked on in awe, her admiration evident in her eyes. Andy finished second, right after Tad.

As Andy and Ruth embraced in the aftermath of his victorious run, he couldn't help but feel a sense of vindication. "See, falling isn't so bad after all," he grinned, his eyes sparkling with pride.

Ruth replied, "You really fell to your victory."

Tad and his friends approached Andy, and their expressions softened. "Congratulations, Andy," Tad said, extending a hand. "And we're sorry for how we treated you. You really showed us what determination looks like."

Andy shook Tad's hand, a smile spreading across his face. "Thanks, Tad. It means a lot."

Later, as they returned home, Ruth reflected on the day's events. The lessons learned and the victories achieved left an indelible mark on both of them. With a newfound appreciation for resilience and determination, they looked forward to facing whatever challenges lay ahead, knowing that together they could overcome anything.

So readers, hope you learned something important from Andy's story. In any competition, it's important to have fun and whatever you do, always give 100%.

Unless you're donating blood.

Okay tell me, what's common between the apple that fell on Newton's head and Andy ?

 I don't know.

One fell for discovery, the other for victory!

Zuri's Comet

Zuri could hardly contain her excitement as she packed her bags for another summer at Grandpa's house. She carefully folded her favorite T-shirts, the ones with bright colors and fun patterns that she always wore on adventures. She tucked her well-worn journal into a side pocket, the pages already filled with sketches and stories from previous summers. Zuri made sure to pack her lucky baseball cap, the one Grandpa had given her when she was just six years old. She even included a new sketchbook and a set of colored pencils, excited about the new memories and drawings she would create.

But as she skipped downstairs, her happiness quickly faded at the sight of her family gathered with serious faces.

"Hey, what's going on?" Zuri asked, her eyes wide with curiosity.

Her mom sighed softly. "Sweetie, we need to talk."

Confusion wrinkled Zuri's nose as she looked from her mom to her dad, who sat quietly at the kitchen table. "Is something wrong?" she asked, feeling a tiny knot of worry in her belly.

Her parents shared a look before her dad spoke up gently. "Zuri, we have some not-so-great news about Grandpa. His house might be in trouble because of his financial situation."

The words hung in the air, casting a shadow over Zuri's excitement. Her heart sank as she realized their special place might be lost. "But can't we help Grandpa?" she asked, her voice small and shaky.

Her parents exchanged a look filled with sadness. "We wish we could, Zuri," her dad said softly, "but it's not that simple."

They arrived at Grandpa's house, but Zuri skipped dinner, her sadness overwhelming her appetite. She sought comfort in Grandpa's backyard under the starry sky, the place where they had shared so many happy moments.

Grandpa appeared with a bowl of ice cream in one hand and something hidden behind his back. His warm smile lifted Zuri's spirits a little. "Hey, Zuri," he greeted her, his voice as soothing as a lullaby. "I thought we could use a little stargazing tonight. And I brought your favorite treat — ice cream!"

Zuri managed a small smile and accepted the ice cream. "Thanks, Grandpa."

Grandpa revealed a shiny telescope from behind his back, grinning mischievously. "I brought something special, too."

Zuri's eyes widened with delight. "Wow, Grandpa, a telescope! Can we use it tonight?"

"Of course!" Grandpa said. "But first, let's enjoy some ice cream and take in the beauty of the night sky."

As they settled down with their ice cream, the familiar comfort of Grandpa's backyard wrapped around Zuri like a warm hug. She set up her phone to record, thinking about how this might be their last backyard gathering, a place filled with so many cherished memories. She wanted to capture every moment, every laugh, and every story shared under the open sky.

The night was clear, and the stars twinkled brightly above them. The air was cool, carrying the scent of blooming flowers and freshly cut grass. Zuri took a deep breath, savoring the peacefulness that always seemed to accompany their stargazing nights.

Just as they were enjoying their treats, a strange hush fell over the backyard. The familiar sounds of crickets chirping and leaves rustling seemed to fade away, replaced by an almost electric stillness. Zuri looked up, puzzled, as the entire sky began to turn a brilliant shade of blue, as if someone had flipped a switch and filled the night with daylight.

A streak of light suddenly shot across the sky, splitting it in two with dazzling brilliance. The light was so intense that it cast long shadows on the ground, illuminating the backyard with an otherworldly glow. "It's a shooting star!" Zuri yelled, her voice a mix of excitement and awe. She quickly closed her eyes and made a wish, her heart pounding with the thrill of the moment.

But the spectacle didn't end there. As Zuri opened her eyes, she saw that the sky had come alive with movement. Dozens of meteors began to streak across the sky, each one leaving a trail of shimmering light behind. It was as if the universe had decided to put on a show just for them.

Grandpa was equally stunned, his usually calm demeanor giving way to a look of pure awe. "I've never seen anything like this," he whispered, his voice barely audible over the quiet hum of the night. They both sat there, spellbound, watching the sky burn with the fiery trails of the meteors.

Zuri's phone, set up earlier, perfectly captured the ethereal dance of the meteors in the night sky.

The next day, as the sun rose over Grandpa's backyard, Zuri eagerly showed her parents the video she had captured of the meteor shower. Their jaws dropped in awe as they watched the dazzling display unfold on Zuri's phone screen.

"Wow, Zuri, this is incredible!" her dad exclaimed, his eyes wide with amazement.

Her mom nodded in agreement, a proud smile spreading across her face. "You've really outdone yourself this time, sweetie. This video is going to be something special. "Encouraged by her parents' reactions, Zuri eagerly posted the video on social media, her heart fluttering with excitement as she awaited the world's response, eager to see how they would react to the magical spectacle she had captured.

Soon, a local newspaper reported about the video, and it became so popular that Zuri and her grandpa were invited to a local news channel.

During the interview, the anchor asked, "What did you wish for in the video? We saw you closing your eyes."

Zuri explained, "I wished for my grandpa's house to be saved. This might have been one of our last memories in the backyard due to his financial problems."

Her story, much like her video, became the talk of the town. Zuri was thrilled with the recognition she received at school and in her neighborhood.

Being an avid lover of stars and cosmic events, Zuri was filled with excitement about the upcoming appearance of the Pons-Brooks comet, a rare celestial event occurring only once every 71 years. With anticipation building, she decided: she would invite her friends to witness the comet's spectacle from her grandpa's backyard.

Together with her family, Zuri embarked on transforming the backyard into a celestial wonderland fit for the occasion. They adorned every corner with twinkling lights, set up telescopes, and laid out cozy blankets for stargazing. News of Zuri's stargazing event spread like wildfire, igniting curiosity and excitement throughout the community.

On the eagerly awaited day, not only did Zuri's friends gather in the backyard, but also her classmates, teachers, and even strangers from neighboring towns.

Grandpa, with a heart as big as an elephant, welcomed everyone. In no time, the entire backyard was packed. Finally, the moment came, and everyone witnessed the mesmerizing and historic event of the Pons-Brooks comet. Zuri was overjoyed, and Grandpa was proud as their backyard stargazing reached new heights.

But the surprises were not over. The visitors had collectively crowdfunded an amount as a token of appreciation for Zuri and her family. They presented the money to Grandpa, helping to alleviate his financial struggles.

The funds saved Grandpa's house, ensuring that Zuri could enjoy many more summer days and nights under the beautiful skies in his backyard. As they gazed up at the stars, they knew that no matter what the future held, their bond and the magic of their stargazing adventures would remain forever.

Wow, Zuri had the most unforgettable summer ever!

Yeah, seeing a meteor shower and saving Grandpa's house is pretty epic!

Talking of which, did you know she gave away all her comic books after that?

Why would she do that?

Because now she reads only **'comet books'**!

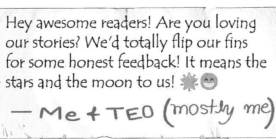

I thought, it's kind of important to ask for feedback.

Yes, but I said not before they read half of the book.

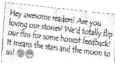

Do you ever get nervous when speaking in front of a crowd? The next story is all about finding a solution to that fear.

Leo, what did I say about spoilers? Leave now.

Nervous
Little Alexa

Once upon a time, there was a girl named Alexa. She was very clever, but also very quiet. She hardly ever spoke, even in class. Alexa's quiet nature often left her on her own among her classmates, except for her one close friend, Kevin. While other kids were outgoing, Alexa preferred to be by herself. However, she wasn't completely alone because Kevin understood and accepted her just as she was. This friendship was essential to Alexa, helping her feel connected to others around her.

There was one more person, and Alexa felt comfortable around her. Her name is Miss Stella Wesley. She was Alexa's favorite teacher and was a warm and encouraging figure in the classroom. Known for her gentle demeanor and insightful teaching methods, she had a unique ability to make each of her students feel valued and understood. Miss Wesley was particularly skilled in English, and she brought the subject to life with her passion and knowledge.

One sunny morning, Miss Wesley announced to her buzzing English class that they would be having a spelling competition. She explained that she would dictate words to the students, who needed to write them down accurately. She also made it clear that she would say each word only twice at most. The competition began, and everyone participated with excitement and enthusiasm. The competition ended, and everyone was excited to see who would win.

The next morning, as Miss Wesley stepped into the classroom, a palpable buzz of excitement greeted her. The students, all on the edge of their seats, watched intently as she walked to the front of the room, holding the much-anticipated results of the spelling competition. Silence fell over the room as she began to speak.

"Guess what, class?" Miss Wesley said, her eyes twinkling. "Alexa got the highest score!" Instantly, the room erupted into applause, with classmates turning towards Alexa, cheering and clapping enthusiastically. Alexa, usually so reserved, blushed and smiled shyly, acknowledging the recognition.

Miss Wesley approached her, her expression one of both surprise and pride. "Well done, Alexa!" she exclaimed, handing her a shiny certificate of achievement.

From that moment on, Miss Wesley took a special interest in Alexa, intrigued and impressed by the quiet girl's hidden talents and academic prowess.

Several weeks after the success of the spelling competition, Miss Wesley decided to shake things up with a new challenge for her English class: a role-play competition. This was in preparation for their upcoming lesson on role play. The classroom was rearranged into a semicircle, creating a stage-like setting at the front where each student would perform. The twist was that each student had to impersonate someone else in the class, and the rest would have to guess who it was.

As the competition unfolded, the room buzzed with laughter and applause. Students took turns transforming into their classmates; their performances were filled with exaggerated gestures and playful banter. The atmosphere was light and enjoyable, but Alexa felt her anxiety mounting with each passing moment.

Her hands were cold and clammy as she nervously twisted them together. She took deep breaths, trying to calm her racing heart and steady her nerves. The time ticked slowly until, inevitably, her name was called. Heart pounding, Alexa slowly stood up. Her legs felt like jelly as she made her way to the front, facing her classmates.

She began her performance with a clear and steady voice, managing to capture everyone's attention. But as she delved deeper, her mind suddenly went blank. The words she had rehearsed vanished, leaving her mute and motionless in front of her peers. She stood frozen, unable to utter another word or move. The room fell into a tense silence, waiting to see if she could recover from the sudden halt.

The room fell silent, the tension palpable. Miss Wesley, standing to the side, gave her a reassuring smile. "It's alright, Alexa," she encouraged warmly. "You made a brave start, take a moment, and when you're ready, you can try again."

The class looked on, waiting to see if she would gather the courage to perform again. The period ended, and Alexa felt relieved.

After everyone had left the classroom, Miss Wesley noticed Alexa looking upset and approached her. "Alexa, what makes you so nervous about speaking in front of everyone?" she asked gently. Alexa tried to speak but couldn't find the words, remaining silent and troubled.

After the school, Alexa trudged home, her heart heavy with disappointment and frustration. Each step felt like a weight pulling her deeper into her sadness. As soon as she entered the house, she brushed past her mother, who greeted her with a warm smile.

"How was school today, sweetie?" her mother asked, noticing Alexa's sullen expression.

Alexa didn't respond. Instead, she walked straight to her room, her silence in stark contrast to her usual politeness. She slammed the door behind her and locked it, collapsing onto her bed in a fit of tears.

Inside her room, she replayed the day's events over and over in her mind. Her performance, the silence, the embarrassment—it all felt unbearable. "Why can't I just be normal?" she whispered to herself, her voice breaking. "Why can't I just talk like everyone else?"

Her mother, sensing something was wrong, gently knocked on the door. "Alexa, can you come downstairs?" she called softly.

"Go away, Mom," Alexa replied, her voice muffled by the pillow she clutched. "I don't want to talk."

"I made your favorite dinner," her mother tried again. "Please come down."

"I said go away!" Alexa shouted, her voice tinged with desperation and anger. "Just leave me alone!"

Her mother sighed, her heart aching for her daughter. "Alright, Alexa," she said gently. "I'll be here if you need me."

But Alexa didn't respond. She curled up on her bed, her tears soaking the pillow. The emotional turmoil drained her, and eventually she fell asleep, her stomach empty and her heart still heavy with the weight of the day's events.

The next day, Miss Wesley, realizing she might not get through to Alexa directly, decided to consult someone who might understand her fears better. She found Kevin in the hallway and pulled him aside. She asked him about Alexa's nervousness.

Kevin shared, "She's always been like this. She thinks others are going to mock her if she speaks."

After recess, it was time for English class. Miss Wesley stood at the front of the room and announced, "Today, I'm going to tell you a story." The kids immediately perked up, leaning forward in their seats, eager to listen.

"There once was a girl who was very talented and smart. She loved to go out and travel to new places," Miss Wesley began.

"Would she go out on her own?" Timmy asked.

"Yes, Timmy. Sometimes by herself, but mostly with her parents." As Miss Wesley told the story, Alexa listened intently. "She excelled in spelling and writing competitions. Despite her many talents, she had one problem: she couldn't talk to anyone—not even her classmates or her teacher."

"But why?" asked Jerry.

"Because she thought if she spoke in front of everyone, they would laugh at her and make fun of her," Miss Wesley explained.

45

Hearing the story, Alexa felt a wave of nervousness wash over her, realizing Miss Wesley was talking about her.

"That's not true," Emily piped up. "People don't laugh at me. They laugh with me because I'm funny!" Everyone laughed along with her.

Miss Wesley smiled and said, "You're right, Emily. I wish she could see it that way and find the courage to speak up. But do you know that the girl I'm talking about is actually among us?"

Alexa felt her heart race, sensing that Miss Wesley was about to reveal her identity. Everyone started looking around, curious to know who the quiet girl was.

"And the name of that girl is... Stella Wesley," Miss Wesley announced. The class was surprised, and Alexa finally looked up, feeling relieved.

"Yes, kids, I used to be very quiet in my class. I was afraid to say even 'Hi' to someone, let alone get on stage to teach such amazing students. But I conquered my fear because I had a lot to say and share."

Finally, the bell rang, and everyone left. As Alexa was about to leave, Miss Wesley asked her to stay back.

"I know there is one more girl who's also very bright and has lots of ideas to share but is afraid to speak up. And it's you," Miss Wesley said gently.

Alexa looked down, feeling embarrassed, and turned to leave. Just then, she finally gathered some courage and hesitantly asked, "Miss Wesley, can I ask you something?"

"Of course," Miss Wesley replied.

"How did you gather the courage to speak?" Alexa asked.

Miss Wesley responded, "I started by speaking to myself in the mirror, then gradually to my dog, and slowly to my parents. In a few days, I had enough courage to talk to my friends. After a lot of practice, I finally started addressing the whole class when given a chance. It took time, but I practiced and practiced until I overcame my fear."

Encouraged by Miss Wesley's journey, Alexa decided to start practicing speaking just like she had. She was motivated to overcome her fears, using her teacher as her role model. At first, she would practice saying simple phrases and sentences, gradually gaining confidence to herself.

Next, she started talking to her pet cat, Ginger, telling her about her day and reading stories aloud. This practice helped Alexa feel more comfortable with the sound of her own voice. Slowly, she began to greet the kids who lived next door, managing a shy "hello" and sometimes even a short conversation.

Alexa made a conscious effort to engage with guests and her parents' friends whenever they visited. She would ask polite questions and respond to their inquiries, even if it was just with a few words at a time. Each small conversation gradually boosted her confidence.

In class, Alexa started participating more. She would raise her hand to answer questions and share her thoughts during group discussions. Although she still felt nervous, she remembered Miss Wesley's advice to practice and persevere.

Over time, Alexa found herself speaking up more and more. Her classmates began to see her not just as the quiet girl, but as someone with interesting ideas and insights. She felt proud of her progress and grateful for Miss Wesley's encouragement. Alexa's journey was gradual, but each small step brought her closer to overcoming her fear and finding her voice.

What a wonderful story. It teaches us that sometimes, the quietest people have the loudest minds.

Yup, Alexa's like a ninja—silent but smart!

Speaking of which, do you know why Miss Wesley had to put on sunglasses when she entered the class?

 Why?

Because her students are so bright!

Minty, a young girl with curly brown hair and bright eyes, loved visiting the library to read picture books. One sunny afternoon, she eagerly stepped into the lift to go to the upper floor, where the children's section of the library awaited her. The lift began to rise, but suddenly, with a jolt, it came to a halt. Minty found herself trapped inside the small, dimly lit lift.

She pressed the buttons to go up and down and even the help button, but nothing worked. Everything seemed to be frozen. Her heart began to pound with fear. She pressed the help button again, harder this time. "Hello? Can anyone hear me? I'm trapped in the lift! Please, help!"

Tears started to well up as she realized she was all alone. Her small frame trembled with each panicked breath.

Inside the library, Tony, the kind-hearted librarian with round glasses perched on his nose, was stocking books on the shelves when he heard Minty's cries echoing from within the closed lift doors. "Help me, somebody, please! I'm trapped here," she cried.

With a furrowed brow, Tony swiftly dialed the maintenance number, his voice urgent as he explained the situation. As Tony waited outside the lift for help to arrive, he glanced at the closed lift doors, his concern growing for Minty, trapped on the other side. "Hey, sweetheart, don't panic; help is on its way," Tony said softly. "What's your name?" he asked gently.

"M-Minty," she replied, her voice trembling.

Understanding the terror of being alone in a small space, Tony decided to share a story with Minty, hoping to distract her from her fear. But he couldn't think of any inspiring stories right away. Just then, he noticed a book in his hand, which read "Harriet Tubman (AKA Minty)." With gentle words, Tony began to weave a tale of bravery and resilience, recounting the story of another young girl named Minty, who faced her fears head-on.

"Minty, that's a wonderful name," Tony remarked softly, his voice calm and soothing. "I know another Minty who faced great trouble, just like you, but she was very brave. Do you want to hear about her?"

Amidst her sobs, Minty hesitated but then replied, "Yes," her voice barely audible through her tears.

Tony smiled softly, his heart warming at Minty's willingness to listen. "Alright then, let me tell you about her. This Minty, also known as Harriet Tubman, was born in the 1820s in Maryland," he began, his tone gentle yet filled with empathy. "She was born into a time when slavery was allowed and people could own other people, just like they owned property."

As Tony spoke, Minty's tears began to ease. "Harriet endured harsh treatment, including physical abuse and scars from beatings," Tony continued, his voice laced with compassion. "But she never gave up hope."

"What happened next?" Minty asked, her voice still shaky but curious, a glimmer of interest shining through her tears.

"At the age of 12, Harriet suffered a severe head injury," Tony explained gently, comforting Minty with his careful words. "But she never gave up. She knew she had to escape to find freedom."

"Did she escape?" Minty inquired, her eyes wide with anticipation.

"Yes, she did," Tony replied with a reassuring smile. "After several attempts, Harriet finally fled Maryland and made it to Philadelphia, where slavery was prohibited. It was like a new beginning for her."

Tony continued the story, his voice growing more passionate. "Harriet began her life as a free woman in Philadelphia, but soon discovered that her niece and two daughters were still enslaved. Determined to rescue them, she made the brave decision to return to Maryland. With the help of allies and the Underground Railroad, she succeeded in freeing many enslaved individuals, including her niece and daughters."

Minty listened intently, her fear momentarily forgotten. "What was the Underground Railroad?" she asked, her curiosity piqued.

"The Underground Railroad wasn't an actual railroad; it was a secret network of people and safe houses," Tony explained gently. "It also had conductors who helped enslaved people like Harriet escape to freedom. Harriet herself became a guide on this secret path, leading people to safety."

"So, she became a conductor too?" Minty asked, her eyes lighting up with newfound understanding.

"Exactly," Tony affirmed, his smile widening. "Harriet was brave and selfless. Even after securing her own freedom, she repeatedly returned to help others escape." He added that his tone was filled with admiration.

Minty's fear gradually melted away as she listened to Tony's tale. "But why did she go back to help others?" she asked, her voice filled with wonder and admiration for Harriet's bravery.

"That's a great question," Tony replied, smiling. "You see, Minty, Harriet didn't just want freedom for herself. She believed that everyone deserved to be free. So even after she found her own freedom, she went back to help others escape from slavery. She was incredibly brave and selfless."

As Tony finished his story, Minty sat in awe, inspired by the bravery and resilience of the other Minty. At that moment, she discovered a newfound strength within herself. "I can be brave too," she whispered, wiping away her remaining tears.

With newfound courage, Minty sat up straighter, her small hands gripping the railing of the lift as she resolved to be brave. Just then, Tony noticed the arrival of the maintenance worker. "Hang tight, Minty. They're here to get you out," he said reassuringly.

The maintenance worker swiftly opened the door to the lift. Minty emerged, her face flushed with relief and gratitude. She rushed into Tony's arms, thanking him wholeheartedly for his kindness. "Thank you for telling me the story," she said, her eyes shining with appreciation.

"You were very brave, Minty," Tony replied, hugging her gently. "And I have a special gift for you." He handed her a copy of the Harriet Tubman book. "This is for you. It's a story of courage and resilience, just like yours."

Minty accepted the book with a grateful smile. "Thank you, Tony. I can't wait to read it."

As they walked to the children's section together, Minty realized that bravery didn't mean not being afraid; it meant facing her fears head-on, just like Harriet Tubman — and just like herself.

In that moment, Minty knew that the library would always be a place where she could find not just stories but strength and courage as well.

Randy was the only child of his parents, a bubbly boy full of energy and laughter. His favorite pastime was playing basketball in the backyard, where he would spend hours shooting hoops and perfecting his dribbling skills. Despite his likable qualities, Randy had one glaring issue: he struggled to control his temper.

More often than not, Randy's anger would flare up over the smallest of things. If he missed a shot or someone accidentally bumped into him, he would lash out in frustration. This pattern of behavior extended to his home life too. After a particularly rough day at school, where Randy had an argument with his teacher over a misunderstood homework assignment, he would come home and unleash his pent-up anger, throwing things around and yelling at his parents. Even their little pet dog, Dodo, would cower in fear, seeking refuge behind the safety of a chair. His mom started to avoid arguing with him, knowing he would flare up quickly.

One day, after a fight with the neighbor's kid, Jimmy, over a basketball game, Randy's dad finally had enough. "Randy, this behavior has to stop," he said sternly.

Randy crossed his arms and rolled his eyes. "Jimmy started it, Dad! He wasn't playing fair!"

"That's no excuse for your outburst," his dad replied, his tone firm. "From now on, whenever you feel angry, I want you to go outside and release your anger there. It's not fair for us or Dodo to be on the receiving end of your outbursts."

"But, Dad, he — " Randy began, but his father cut him off.

"No more excuses, Randy. You have to learn to control yourself," his dad insisted.

Feeling chastised, Randy reluctantly agreed to his dad's request. From that day forward, whenever anger threatened to consume him, Randy would flee to the garden shed and unleash his frustration. He would slam the door shut with all his might and throw things around, the echoes of his anger reverberating in the quiet garden. Oftentimes, Randy would slam the door multiple times.

At first, the approach didn't seem to be working, as there was hardly anyone there to stop Randy from causing damage to the garden shed. Randy's mother grew increasingly concerned about her husband's method. One evening, she voiced her worries. "Do you really think this is helping, dear? I'm afraid that by letting Randy express his anger so aggressively, it might do more harm than good."

His father sighed. "I understand your worries, but he needs to learn to control his anger. Let's give it a bit more time. He might realize the futility of his actions and start looking for better ways to manage his frustration."

As time went by, Randy found himself making the journey to the garden shed less and less frequently. The banging of the door became sporadic, replaced by moments of calm reflection as Randy learned to channel his anger in healthier ways. Sometimes, because the time between him getting angry and banging the door was too much, his anger would melt, and he would come out of the shed without banging the door at all, his frustrations dissipating like clouds on a sunny day.

Eventually, the banging ceased altogether, and Randy's anger became a thing of the past. His parents noticed the positive change in their son and couldn't be prouder of his progress. Randy, too, was proud of himself for overcoming his temper tantrums and making strides towards becoming a better person.

One stormy evening, as Randy and his family were returning home from his uncle's house, disaster struck. The sky darkened ominously, and thunder rumbled in the distance as rain poured down in torrents. Dodo whimpered in fear at the sound of lightning, seeking comfort from Randy's reassuring touch.

As they hurried towards the safety of their home, Randy's dad realized with a sinking feeling that he had forgotten the keys at his brother's house. Panic set in as they realized they were locked out in the midst of a thunderstorm with no shelter in sight.

With no other option, they dashed towards the garden shed, hoping to find refuge from the storm. But as they reached the shed and attempted to open the door, they were met with resistance. The doorknob had been broken, and the door itself was badly damaged from Randy's past outbursts.

Despite the door's sorry state, Randy's dad managed to pry it open, and they huddled inside the shed. Even the light bulb was broken into pieces, and now the whole family would have to stay inside the shed in the dark with water splashing all over them as the door, without its knob, wouldn't stay closed. Randy felt a pang of guilt as he looked around at the damage he had caused.

"This is what happens when anger gets the best of us," his dad said solemnly, gesturing towards the broken door. "Just like this door, our angry words and actions can leave lasting scars on those around us."

Randy hung his head in shame, a newfound understanding dawning on him. "I'm sorry, Dad," he whispered, tears welling up in his eyes. "I never realized the impact of my anger until now."

His dad pulled him into a tight embrace. "It's okay, Randy. The important thing is that you've recognized your mistakes and are committed to doing better moving forward."

As they finally made their way back into the warmth of their home, Randy felt a sense of peace wash over him. The storm may have passed, but the lessons he had learned would stay with him forever. And with his family by his side, he knew that he could weather any storm that came his way.

Wow, what a heartwarming ending to such an emotional story. Randy really learned a lot!

 Ever wonder why Randy eventually stopped going to the garden shed?

 Why ?

 Because he learned that breaking habits is better than breaking doors!

 Make sense !

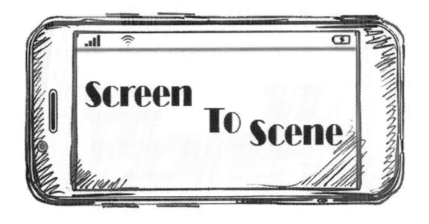

Julia and Ivy were the best of friends, always sticking together despite their differences. Both girls were very pretty, but while Julia loved meeting new people and exploring new places, Ivy preferred playing games and didn't like socializing much.

Their differing views often led to deep discussions. "Ivy, you can't really experience the world through a screen," Julia would argue passionately. "Meeting people and seeing places with your own eyes is unmatched."

Ivy, glued to her phone, would counter, "But you can see everything on your phone! Have you seen the pyramids in real life? No, but you've seen them on your phone. Everything you need is right here."

Frustrated, Julia would respond, "Ivy, the real world is so much more vibrant. Talking to people face-to-face is important for growing as a person." But Ivy, putting on her headphones, would cut her off, signaling the end of the debate.

Despite their differences, they remained inseparable. Excited about spending time together, they decided to join a week- long summer camp during their vacation. Both were thrilled as they prepared for the adventure, packing everything they thought might need and arriving at the designated meeting spot on time.

On the journey to the camp, Julia quickly made friends and introduced Ivy to them. Julia joined in on games and laughter, while Ivy remained engrossed in her tablet. The bus was filled with chatter, and Julia was in the center of it, sharing stories and jokes. "Hey Ivy, meet Emma and Noah. They're super cool!"

"Hi," Ivy mumbled, barely glancing up from her screen.

Meanwhile, Ivy's attention was fixated on her phone as she updated her status and checked her social media notifications and new digital game. She barely looked up as they got off the bus. "Look, Ivy," Julia said, pointing towards a group of kids playing a game of tag. "Isn't it great? So many new people to meet!"

Ivy shrugged, her eyes never leaving her screen. "I guess. But I've got my game here. It's pretty engaging too."

After a lengthy journey, they finally arrived at the campsite and enjoyed a well-deserved evening snack. The campsite was set in a beautiful clearing surrounded by tall trees. The smell of pine filled the air, and the sound of a nearby stream added to the serene atmosphere. Julia was thrilled and couldn't wait to explore.

The camp was bustling with activity, hosting around fifty students. Julia's eyes lit up with joy at the sight of so many potential new friends. She saw groups of kids chatting excitedly, counselors organizing games, and a lively buzz all around. The campgrounds were filled with laughter and energy, making Julia's heart race with excitement.

After dinner, everyone got busy setting up their tents. Julia and Ivy worked together and did such an impressive job that it caught the attention of others. People came by to compliment them. "Wow, you two did a great job with your tent!" said one of the camp counselors.

"Thanks," Ivy replied politely, then retreated to the tent to check the comments on her recently posted photos. Julia, energized by the interactions, offered to help anyone struggling with their tent.

"Need a hand?" she asked a group of younger kids who were wrestling with their tent poles.

"Yes, please!" they replied, grateful for her assistance.

The real adventure began the next morning with hiking, followed by trekking on the third day and a visit to a nearby zoo on the fourth. Ivy focused on vlogging and creating short videos of outdoor locations. "Hey guys, check out this amazing view from the hiking trail," she narrated into her phone, capturing the scenery.

In contrast, Julia spent her time participating in games, cooking, singing, and dancing. She loved the communal meals where everyone pitched in and the campfires where they sang songs and shared stories. She felt a sense of belonging and joy that Ivy seemed to miss.

The next day, the teachers allowed everyone to explore the surrounding areas. Many students invited Julia to join their groups, eager for her company, but no one extended the same invitation to Ivy. Loyal as ever, Julia chose to stay with Ivy, promising the others she would join them the following day. Together, they ventured into the jungle, curious and adventurous, straying further than planned.

As they walked deeper into the dense forest, Julia began to worry. "Ivy, I think we might be lost," she said, panic creeping into her voice.

Ivy confidently reassured her, pulling out her tablet. "Don't worry, with this thing in my hand, we can't get lost." She opened the maps, but the signal was weak. "Fear not," Ivy said. "I have an offline map app." Delighted when it worked, Ivy started navigating.

Julia followed Ivy deeper into the jungle. However, the tablet suddenly stopped working. "Oh no, my tablet is dead!" Ivy exclaimed, panic setting in.

Julia's heart raced as she tried to stay calm. "Remember what Tim said? There are white marks on the trees that lead back to the campsite. Let's look for them."

They separated to scan the area. Ivy's breath quickened, her usual confidence waning. "What if we can't find any marks, Julia?"

"Stay positive, Ivy. We will find them," Julia reassured her. Moments later, Ivy shouted, "Found it!" after spotting a white mark. Relieved, they started following the white marks back towards the camp.

Every few steps, Ivy would pause and ask, "Are you sure this is the right way?"

"I remember what Tim said. It's definitely the white marks," Julia would respond, her voice steady but her heart pounding.

As they frantically walked, Ivy suddenly spotted a long, black snake near her foot. "Oh my God!" she screamed, freezing in fear.

Julia, startled but remembering the zoo visit, said, "Stay still, Ivy. Snakes won't harm us if we don't provoke them." They watched quietly as the snake slithered away.

Far in the distance, they saw smoke rising from a bonfire. "We're almost there!" Julia exclaimed.

Julia and Ivy practically ran in the direction of the bonfire. But when they finally arrived, they realized it wasn't their camp at all—it was a different one! The campsite was eerily quiet, with only the faint crackling of the fire.

"Julia, what do we do now?" Ivy whispered, her fear evident in her voice.

Julia took a deep breath. "The fire seems fresh. Whoever was here can't be far. Let's look around." They decided to split up and search for help. "Anyone out here? Please help!" they called out.

Ivy spotted a group of older students in the distance. Gathering her courage, she approached them but struggled to explain their situation. "Um, we're lost... and, uh..."

One of the students noticed her distress. "Are you okay? Do you need help?"

Julia arrived, taking charge. "Excuse me, we ventured too far into the forest and lost our way. We're not sure how to get back to our camp. Can you please help us find our way back?"

"Sure," one of the students said, pulling out a flashlight. "We have a map. We can guide you back."

The students, concerned and kind, quickly helped them find their way back, using a torch and a paper map. As they walked, one of the older students chatted with Ivy. "It's easy to get lost out here. You're lucky you found us."

Ivy nodded, still shaken but grateful. "Thank you so much. We really appreciate it."

When they finally reached their campsite, everyone was relieved to see Julia and Ivy. The camp had been searching for them. "Thank goodness you two are back," a counselor sighed in relief.

Julia thanked the group for their help, and Ivy, feeling a bit guilty, realized the importance of socializing and paying attention to their surroundings. She understood that phones and tablets couldn't replace real-life experiences and connections.

"I think I'll try to be more social from now on and spend less time on my phone," Ivy admitted to Julia later that night. "Today showed me how important it is to know the actual world along with the virtual one."

Julia smiled, hugging her friend. "I'm glad, Ivy. We'll have so many more adventures together."

And from that day forward, Ivy tried to balance her love for technology with the real-world experiences that Julia cherished. Their friendship grew even stronger, enriched by the lessons they learned together in the heart of the forest.

So, readers, Julia and Ivy's story reminds us that sometimes getting lost helps you find what really matters.

 And you know why Julia didn't mind helping everyone with their tents?

Why ?

 Because she was intent on making new friends!

Haha, very funny... my stomach hurts from laughing so much...

One sunny morning, Mia spotted a phone booth on the street; its red paint faded with time. Intrigued, she quickened her pace, her eyes lighting up with curiosity. The booth stood as a relic of a bygone era, a portal to the past in the midst of the bustling city.

Approaching the booth, Mia fumbled through her pockets, her fingers searching for the necessary coins. With a triumphant grin, she produced a handful of change and approached the shopkeeper, Mr. Thompson, who stood watchful beside the booth.

"Excuse me, sir," Mia addressed him politely. "May I use the phone booth, please?"

Mr. Thompson, a kindly man with a twinkle in his eye, nodded in assent. "Of course, go ahead."

As Mia stepped into the booth, she couldn't shake the feeling of anticipation that thrummed through her veins. It was as if every coin she dropped into the slot brought her closer to a pivotal moment.

Meanwhile, Tina, Mr. Thompson's daughter, observed Mia's every move with keen interest from her perch behind the counter. She watched as Mia inserted the coins and dialed a number with trembling fingers; her curiosity was piqued by the intensity of Mia's expression.

With bated breath, Mia waited for the call to connect, her heart hammering in her chest. When a voice finally crackled through the receiver, Mia's nerves flared, but she pushed past her apprehension and spoke with determination.

"Hello, is this the Delight Bakery? " Mia inquired, her voice tinged with nervousness.

"Yes, it is," came the reply, followed by, "How may I assist you today?"

"I'd like to speak to the manager, please," Mia requested, her voice steady despite the butterflies in her stomach.

"This is Mrs. Clinton, the manager and owner of the bakery," Mrs. Clinton replied, her voice warm and welcoming.

Mia's pulse quickened as she realized she was speaking directly to the person in charge. Gathering her courage, she launched into her spiel, expressing her heartfelt interest in the baker position.

"My name is Emily, and I'm genuinely passionate about baking. I'm eager to apply for the baker position at your bakery," Mia explained earnestly. "I'm willing to work extra hours, take on night shifts, and even accept lower wages if given the chance to showcase my skills."

"Thank you, Emily," Mrs. Clinton said, her tone warm and understanding. "Your passion for baking shines through, and I appreciate your dedication. Unfortunately, we've already found someone for the position who's very good at what she's doing. "As the call ended, a proud smile spread across Mia's face.

As Mia rushes out of the booth, her heart races with anticipation. She's filled with a newfound sense of determination, eager to take on the world.

However, before she can fully process her next move, Mr. Thompson's voice calls out behind her, a blend of concern and urgency. "Miss, wait!" he calls, his footsteps quickening as he tries to catch up to her.

But Mia is already in motion; her mind is focused on the path ahead. She darts through the crowded streets, weaving between pedestrians and dodging obstacles with agility. She can hear Mr. Thompson's voice growing fainter and fainter.

Behind her, Mr. Thompson and Tina are in hot pursuit, their voices echoing in the air as they call out to her. They navigate the crowded streets with determination, their eyes fixed on Mia's fleeting figure ahead.

Finally, Mia skids to a stop in front of the Delight Bakery, her chest heaving with exhaustion. Sweat beads on her forehead as she takes a moment to catch her breath, her lungs burning from the exertion.

But there's no time to rest. With renewed resolve, Mia pushes open the doors of the bakery and hurries inside. The familiar scent of freshly baked goods fills her senses, grounding her in the present moment.

Without hesitation, Mia heads straight to the nearest workstation and rolls up her sleeves. She wastes no time in getting to work, her hands moving with practiced precision as she starts decorating a cake with intricate designs.

As Mia loses herself in the rhythm of her craft, a sense of peace washes over her. With each stroke of icing, she pours her heart into creating something beautiful, a testament to her passion and dedication.

As Mia hurriedly works on the cake, her hands moving with practiced ease, she senses a presence behind her. Turning around, she sees Mr. Thompson standing in the doorway of the bakery, his eyes scanning the room until they land on her. Panic flashes across Mia's face as she fears he might reveal her secret to Mrs. Clinton.

Mr. Thompson and Mia shared a brief moment of connection as their eyes met. Mr. Thompson was about to say something when the approach of the middle-aged lady to the counter diverted his attention.

"Welcome to the Delight Bakery; how may I help you today?" She says it with a warm smile.

Mr. Thompson reads the nameplate of the lady and says, "Mrs. Clinton..." She nods with acknowledgment, and Mr. Thompson's smile grows as if he has solved a puzzle. "Can I please have your bakery's special pastries?" he requests. "Certainly," Mrs. Clinton responds, turning to retrieve the pastries from the cupboard. But before she can fetch them, Mr. Thompson interjects, "Actually, I'd like the one that she's preparing." He points toward Mia.

Meanwhile, Tina watches the interaction with growing confusion, trying to piece together the unfolding events.

Worried and uncertain of Mr. Thompson's intentions, Mia continues to work diligently. Suddenly, Mr. Thompson draws her attention once again. "This pastry looks and smells amazing," he remarks, taking a bite. "I can say for sure, Mrs. Clinton, that not only the pastry but the baker behind it is also very special. You're lucky to have such a fine baker."

"I'm glad you think so," Mrs. Clinton responds with a smile, and Mia finally feels a sense of relief wash over her.

Mr. Thompson and Tina stepped out of the Delight Bakery, each holding a pastry in hand. The warm aroma of freshly baked goods lingered in the air as they made their way down the bustling street.

"Daddy, I'm still confused," Tina said, furrowing her brow. "Why did you run after that girl earlier?"

Mr. Thompson paused, considering Tina's question. "Well, sweetheart," he began, "I thought she needed a job, and I also wanted to hire someone for our shop."

"But if she already has a job, why did she apply for another one at the same Delight Bakery?" Tina asked, her curiosity piqued.

Mr. Thompson smiled, realizing it was time to impart a valuable lesson to his daughter. "You see, Tina," he explained, "sometimes people want to know if they're truly valued in their current position. By calling as she did, the girl was trying to find out if her boss appreciated her work enough to keep her."

Tina's eyes widened in understanding. "So, she was checking if she could be replaced?" she asked.

"Exactly." Mr. Thompson nodded. "And when her boss declined to hire someone else, it showed that she's highly regarded for her skills and dedication."

Tina grinned, the pieces of the puzzle finally falling into place. "This is how you can recognize how special you are." she exclaimed, excited to have learned something new.

Mr. Thompson ruffled Tina's hair affectionately. "That's right, sweetheart," he said. "It's important to know your own worth and to make sure others recognize it too."

What a wonderful lesson about knowing your own worth, wasn't it, Teo ?

I can't stop thinking about the pastries Mia made. I bet they would go perfectly with a hot coffee.

Speaking of coffee, What do you call sad coffee?

What ?

A despresso !

91

Brian
And His Puppy

Once upon a time, there was a young boy named Brian who was on his way home from school. As he walked, he noticed a small puppy in the middle of the road. She seemed lost and frightened, aimlessly wandering without any direction. Seeing the puppy in such distress, Brian felt compelled to do something. He cautiously approached the puppy, gently picked her up, and decided to take her home to ensure she was safe

"What's your name, good girl? Honey? Bravo? Charlie? ... huh, Luna?" Brian suggested trying different names. Hearing "Luna," the puppy barked cutely.

"Oh, you like Luna! Hey, Luna, do you want to come with me?" Brian added it with a smile. Luna barked again, as if to say yes.

Without a care in the world, Brian carried Luna in his arms, talking to her soothingly as he made his way home. The puppy's soft fur and gentle warmth made him feel like he had a new best friend.

When Brian's mother saw him holding the puppy, she was surprised. "Where did you find her?" she asked.

Brian explained, "I found Luna alone and scared in the middle of the road. She looked so lost, Mom. Can we keep her? Please?"

His mother looked concerned. "Brian, she might have an owner who's missing her."

"But Mom, she was in danger on the busy road. She could have been hurt if I hadn't picked her up," Brian pleaded.

Understanding the situation, his mother sighed. "Alright, Brian. Luna can stay, but we need to clean her first. She might be dirty."

Brian agreed eagerly. "Thanks, Mom! I'll wash her right away."

Brian carefully washed Luna, making sure she was clean and safe to bring inside. He gave Luna some food, and the little dog gobbled it up quickly, showing just how hungry she was. His mother offered Luna even more food to ensure she was well-fed. That night, Luna, now feeling safe and cared for, slept alongside Brian, finding comfort in her new friend's presence.

In just a week, Brian and Luna became inseparable best friends. Each day, as Brian came back from school, Luna would be excitedly waiting at the door to greet him. They enjoyed snacks together and spent plenty of time playing in the garden. On rainy days, they found comfort in each other's company, cuddling on the sofa while watching TV, sharing a special bond that only grew stronger with each passing day.

One day, Brian and Luna were playing and having a lot of fun. Suddenly, Luna saw a big dog across the road and ran after it really fast. Brian got scared and ran after Luna, trying to get her to come back. He yelled, "Luna, no! Bad dog, come back!" but Luna didn't listen at all and kept running towards the big dog.

Brian was surprised when he saw Luna run up to the big dog and start playing with it. Luna was so happy, jumping around and wagging her tail. Brian had never seen Luna act like this with other dogs. He tried to get Luna to come back home with him, but Luna wouldn't listen. Feeling upset and helpless, Brian began to cry.

Brian's mom noticed him crying and came over to find out what had happened. "Brian, what's wrong?" she asked, kneeling beside him.

"Luna ran off to play with that big dog, and she won't listen to me," Brian explained, tears streaming down his face.

His mom took a closer look at both dogs and noticed they looked very similar. "Brian, I think the big dog might be Luna's mother," she said gently.

Just then, the person who owned the big dog came over. They seemed in a hurry and took the big dog away quickly.

After everything that happened, Brian and his mom walked back home with Luna. Brian was still upset and puzzled about why Luna hadn't listened to him earlier. When they got home, Luna seemed really sad and wouldn't eat anything. She missed her mother. Brian's mom tried to explain, "Brian, the big dog was Luna's mother. It's natural for Luna to want to be with her."

However, Brian was too upset and didn't want to hear any explanations. The next morning, Brian woke up and noticed something was wrong; his mother wasn't at home. He searched the house, calling her name, but there was no answer. A wave of panic washed over him as he realized his mother was missing.

Brian's father also searched and couldn't find her. Together, they tried calling her cell phone, but it just rang with no answer. As the day went on with no sign of her return, Brian felt increasingly lost and helpless.

"Dad, where could Mom be? She wouldn't go without telling us," Brian said, worry evident in his voice.

"I don't know, Brian. She usually leaves a note or calls. It's strange," his father replied, trying to stay calm but clearly concerned.

With his mother gone, Brian found it hard to manage even simple tasks. He missed her comforting presence, her advice, and her warm smile, which made everything seem okay. Things like making breakfast or finding his school books felt incredibly difficult without her around to guide him.

Brian's worry grew. He couldn't stop thinking about where his mother might be and whether she was safe. The house felt unusually quiet and empty without her laughter and loving words filling the rooms.

"Dad, do you think Mom went to Grandma's house?" Brian asked, his voice trembling.

"I don't think so, Brian. She usually tells us if she's going there," his father said, trying to reassure him but clearly struggling with his own fears. "But let's stay strong and hope she'll come back soon."

As Brian waited anxiously for his mother to return, he noticed Luna lying by the door, looking just as sad and lost.

"Luna, do you miss your mom too?" Brian asked, sitting down beside her. Luna looked up at him with her big, sorrowful eyes and gave a small whimper.

"I know how you feel," Brian said softly, stroking her fur. "I miss my mom too. It's hard, isn't it?"

While Brian was feeling particularly sad, he suddenly heard a familiar voice outside. He rushed to the door and swung it open, only to find his mother standing there. Overcome with relief and happiness, Brian wrapped his arms around her in a tight hug, tears of joy streaming down his face. All his worries disappeared as he felt grateful and happy that she was back home safely.

Interestingly, Brian's father had known all along where his mother was but had acted unaware. He did this to teach Brian a lesson about how hard it would be for Luna to live without her mother, mirroring Brian's own feelings of missing his mom.

The next day, reflecting on his own feelings of loss, Brian understood something important about Luna. He and his mother went to the farmer's house, where Luna's mother was. When Luna saw her mother, she ran to her immediately, clearly overjoyed.

Brian and his mother spoke to the farmer, asking if Luna could stay with her mother. The farmer was kind and agreed to their request. He even told Brian that he was welcome to come and visit Luna at any time. This experience taught Brian a valuable lesson: sometimes, you have to let go of the ones you love for their own happiness.

And so, Brian learned a great deal about love and selflessness from his time with Luna. He visited her often at the farmer's house, and each visit was filled with joy and love. Brian realized that true friendship sometimes means making hard choices for the sake of those we care about, and that love often involves letting go.

.

Hey kids! What an adventurous and heartwarming story about Brian and Luna. Did you enjoy it?

Definitely! Brian's dad deserves the 'Best Actor in a Drama' award for his performance!

Speaking of Dads with acting abilities, what do you think Brian's dad would be called if he finally paid off his house?

Hmm, I don't know... a Good Dad?

Nope, you'd call him... Mortgage Freeman!

The interschool soccer tournament had reached its climax, with Ronny and Rocky's team riding an unbeaten streak all the way to the final. As the final match approached, excitement buzzed through the air like electricity. Ronny and Rocky, best friends and star players of their team, stood at the forefront as the 1st and 2nd highest goal scorers, with Rocky proudly holding the top spot.

But as the tension mounted before the final showdown, cracks began to appear in their team's unity. In the locker room, where camaraderie usually thrives, an argument erupted like a sudden storm.

Ronny looked upset, crossing his arms. "I don't get why everyone's so excited about your goals, Rocky. I've scored a bunch too, you know."

Rocky replied, getting louder. "Yeah, but who's got the most goals in the tournament? Me. I'm the top scorer, Ronny."

Ronny frowned at Rocky. "You wouldn't even be a top scorer if I didn't pass to you so many times!"

Rocky snapped back, sounding frustrated. "Oh, come on! I'm the one who scores when you pass!"

Their teammates exchanged worried glances, sensing the growing animosity between their star players.

As the game kicked off, Ronny and Rocky's minds were still clouded with the argument they had in the locker room.

Determined to prove themselves as superior scorers, they both opted to play as strikers, disregarding their usual teamwork. With each possession, they dribbled fiercely towards the goal, ignoring their teammates' calls for passes.

Despite their individual efforts, Ronny and Rocky found themselves repeatedly foiled by the opposing team's defense. Their attempts at solo goals resulted in missed shots and missed opportunities. The frustration mounted with each failed attempt, but neither player was willing to concede.

Coach Mr. Peter observed the unfolding drama from the sidelines, his concern growing with each passing minute. During the drinks break, he addressed Ronny and Rocky, urging them to set aside their differences for the sake of the team. "You two need to work together," he implored. "We're already behind by 2-0, and we can't afford to keep playing like this."

However, his words seemed to fall on deaf ears as Ronny and Rocky stubbornly persisted in their solo endeavors. Their refusal to cooperate allowed the opposing team to capitalize on their discord. Sensing the disunity among the forwards, the opposing team's defenders tightened their grip, intercepting passes and launching swift counterattacks.

In just a few minutes, the opposing team capitalized on Ronny and Rocky's lack of teamwork. Finding openings in the defense created by the isolated forwards, they swiftly scored two additional goals.

Disappointment weighed heavily on Mr. Peter's heart as he watched his team shuffle back into the locker room, their spirits deflated by the 4-0 score against them. With a solemn expression, he motioned for Ronny and Rocky to remain seated while the rest of the team filed out.

"Boys, we need to talk." Coach Peter's voice held a hint of sternness. "I've had enough. If you two can't settle your differences right now, you'll be staying in this locker room for the rest of the match."

Ronny folded his arms tightly, his face etched with frustration. "It's not all on me," he grumbled.

Rocky shook his head adamantly, his annoyance evident. "No, it's your fault! You never pass the ball!"

"How many times have you passed?" Ronny retorted, his voice sharp with irritation.

Seeing that his words were falling on deaf ears, Mr. Peter let out a heavy sigh. With a heavy heart, he stepped out of the room, locking the door behind him. But the intensity of Ronny and Rocky's argument kept them from noticing his departure.

Ronny glanced around the room, a sense of confinement settling over him. "Did he really lock us in here?" he questioned, his voice tinged with uncertainty.

Rocky nodded, his expression filled with concern. "I can't believe this."

With a sense of urgency, Ronny checked the door, confirming that it was indeed locked. "Now what?" he asked, a note of panic creeping into his voice.

Rocky scanned the room until his gaze landed on the window. "The game's about to start," he reminded Ronny. "We need to find a way out."

Their eyes met as a glimmer of hope sparked between them. "I'll boost you up," Ronny offered, determination shining in his eyes.

With a nod of agreement, Rocky and Ronny positioned a nearby bench beneath the window. Ronny climbed onto the bench first and then hoisted Rocky onto his shoulders, allowing him to reach the window. "I'll get you out," Rocky promised as he squeezed through the narrow opening.

With a sense of urgency, Rocky dashed to the front door of the locker room and swung it open, gesturing for Ronny to follow. Without hesitation, they sprinted out onto the field, their hearts pounding with adrenaline as they realized the game had already begun without them.

Breathless, they approached Coach Peter, their faces flushed with embarrassment. "We're sorry, Coach," Rocky panted, his voice earnest. "We'll play as a team from now on."

Coach Peter nodded, his expression softening with understanding. "Good. Get out there and show them what you're made of."

With renewed determination, Ronny and Rocky rejoined their teammates on the field. This time, their movements were synchronized, their passes were precise, and their teamwork was seamless. As they dribbled past the opposition's defense, they scored goal after goal, closing the gap until the score was tied at 4-4.

With only five minutes remaining, tension gripped the stadium as both teams fought tooth and nail for victory.

Then, in a moment of brilliance, Ronny skillfully maneuvered past the defenders and prepared to take the shot. But at the last second, the opposing goalkeeper intercepted the ball, threatening to dash their hopes of victory.

Remaining calm under pressure, Ronny swiftly passed the ball to Rocky, who expertly nudged it past the goalkeeper and into the goal. The stadium erupted into cheers as the final whistle blew, signaling their miraculous comeback and securing a win for their team.

Amidst the jubilant celebrations, Coach Peter couldn't help but smile, his heart filled with pride for his team. This victory served as a powerful reminder of the importance of teamwork, demonstrating that together, they were capable of achieving greatness beyond their individual talents.

Thank you!

First of all, thank you for reading the book, young reader. I hope you enjoyed the story as much as I enjoyed writing it.

We began with an angry young man, met Alexa and her nervousness, and journeyed with friends like Andy, Brian, and Minty, all while learning valuable lessons. These stories were close to my heart, and I hope you enjoyed reading them as much as we enjoyed writing them.

Stories thrive when shared, so I would be genuinely grateful if you could leave an honest review on Amazon. Your feedback is invaluable to us. Just as flowers rely on bees to spread their pollen, our stories blossom through the support of wonderful readers like you. Thank you for being a part of this journey.

The End of the Road

Remember, being brave and kind, like the heroes in these tales, is what makes you a true hero in real life. Stay courageous and righteous, and perhaps one day, you'll be the amazing person whose unique and incredible story we get to share with the world.

Until then, keep believing in the magic of stories and the hero inside you.

Minty

Luna

★

★

Julia

★

Alexa

Teo

Leo

★

Rocky and Ronny

★

Andy

Mia

Brian

Made in the USA
Las Vegas, NV
03 December 2024

13315716R00063